P9-CER-942

Unraveling
FIBERS

For Mike, with love

Thanks, thanks to thee, my worthy friend,
   For the lesson thou has taught!
Thus at the flaming forge of life
   Our fortunes must be wrought;
Thus on its sounding anvil shaped
   Each burning deed and thought!

   —HENRY WADSWORTH LONGFELLOW
   "The Village Blacksmith"

Atheneum Books for Young Readers
An imprint of Simon & Schuster Children's Publishing Division
1230 Avenue of the Americas
New York, New York 10020

Text and illustrations copyright © 1995 by Patricia A. Keeler and Francis X. McCall, Jr.

The text of this book is set in Simoncini Garamond.

First edition
10 9 8 7 6 5 4 3 2 1
Printed in Hong Kong

Library of Congress Cataloging-in-Publication Data
Keeler, Patricia A.
  Unraveling fibers / by Patricia A. Keeler and Francis X. McCall, Jr.—1st ed.
    p.   cm.   Includes index.
  ISBN 0–689–31777–8
  1. Textile fibers—Juvenile literature.   [1. Fibers.
  2. Textiles.]   I. McCall, Francis X.   II. Title
  TS1540.K44 1995
  677—dc20   93-13906

The photograph on the half-title page
is of Angora rabbits and picked cotton.

Unraveling
FIBERS

PATRICIA A. KEELER
and
FRANCIS X. McCALL, JR.

ATHENEUM BOOKS FOR YOUNG READERS

CONTENTS

WHAT IS A FIBER?

Almost all of your clothes are made of fibers. So are your sheets, towels, curtains, and rugs. Fibers are thin threads. The hairs on your head are fibers. Like human hair, all fibers are straight or curly, smooth or coarse.

There are many different kinds of fibers found in nature that can be made into cloth. Cloth has been created from the silk spiders spin for their webs, from the fur of long-haired family cats, and even from asbestos rocks! All the fibers gathered from plants and animals are called *natural fibers,* but only about a dozen of these are commonly used for cloth.

Other fibers made by chemists are called *synthetic fibers.* These fibers originate with trees, petroleum, and natural gas.

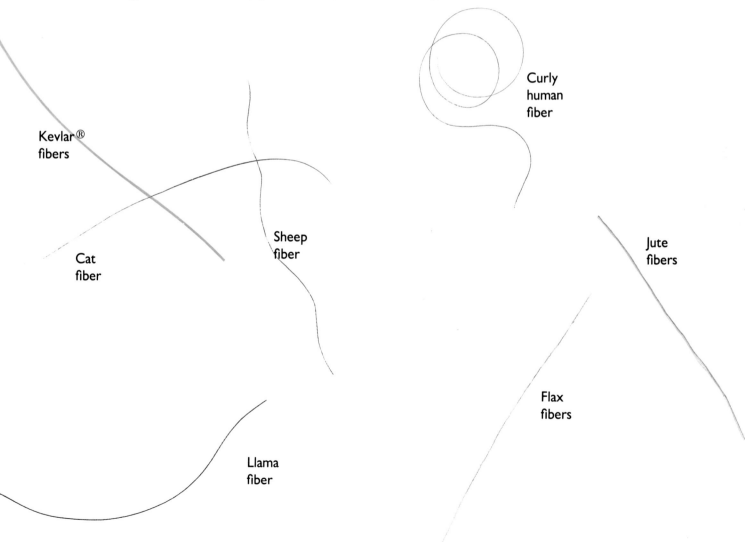

Kevlar® fibers

Curly human fiber

Cat fiber

Sheep fiber

Jute fibers

Flax fibers

Llama fiber

FROM FIBERS TO CLOTH

Natural fibers often grow stuck together or knotted around each other in a mass. Short synthetic fibers become entwined when they are bundled into bales. To make cloth, the fibers must first be untangled. Combing the fibers separates them and makes them lie parallel one to another. Pulling fibers across rows of wire teeth to comb them is called *carding*. Carding can be done by hand or machine.

Two or more types of fibers can be carded together. Carding is a common way to mix fibers. These fiber mixtures are called *blends*.

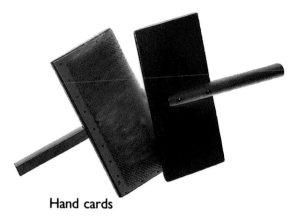

Hand cards

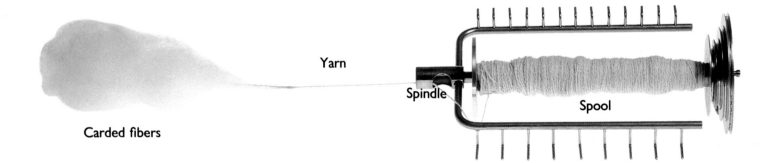

Carded fibers

Yarn

Spindle

Spool

Fibers are fine and may break easily. Many are short. Because of this, they must be twisted together to make yarn strong enough and long enough for cloth. Most fibers are twisted into yarn with *spindles*. The picture above shows a spindle with carded fibers going into it. The spindle turns around and around, twisting, or spinning, the loose fibers into yarn. The yarn is wound onto a spool.

Spindle
and
spool

Spinning wheel

Factory spinning

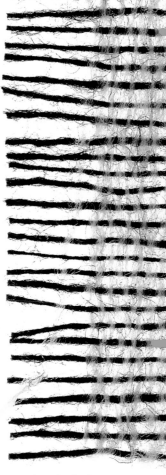

Woven cloth

When a spindle and a spool are made to spin around by turning a wheel, the machine is called a *spinning wheel*. In factories, yarn is spun on rows of machines and wound onto spools.

Yarn can be woven or knitted to make cloth. Woven cloth is made on a *loom*. This is done by crossing one set of yarns over and under another set of yarns. *Warp* yarns run the length of a loom, and *weft* yarns are woven across its width.

Weaving on factory looms

Knitted cloth

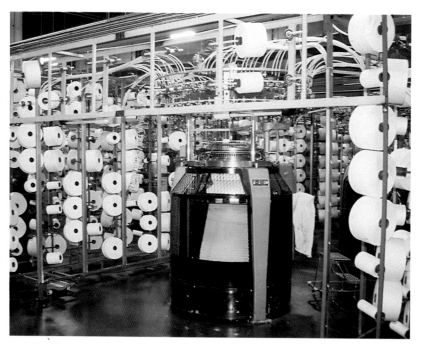

Factory knitting machine

Knitted cloth can be made by hand with knitting needles or on a knitting machine. The yarn is looped through itself row after row. The loops let the cloth stretch. Biking, running, and swimming are easier in stretchy clothes. That is why knitted cloth is used to make exercise clothing, socks, and underwear.

Knitting with knitting needles

FLAX

Linen cloth is made of fibers from the flax plant. It is believed that linen is the first cloth ever made. Pieces of linen have been found that date back to 8000 B.C. Today linen is used to make tableclothes, dish towels, and clothing.

The thin, willowy flax plant grows best where the weather is cool and rainy. Most of the world's flax fibers come from Russia. The finest linen comes from flax raised in Belgium.

Flax seeds are planted in the early spring. Two months later, dainty white or blue flowers open on the slender flax stalks. The flowers bloom for only a day, leaving tiny green seedpods in their place. Soon the flax plants reach three feet tall. Farmers know it is time to gather the flax plants when the stalks start to yellow and the seedpods rattle in the wind.

Flax plants are pulled out of the ground. They are uprooted by hand or with a pulling machine. The plants are piled in stacks to dry.

Pulling machine harvesting flax

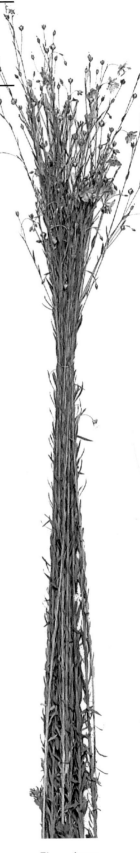

Flax plants

Look closely to see a bundle of flax plants retting in a pond.

Then the flax plants are *retted*. Retting is done by leaving pulled flax plants lying in fields to catch the morning dew, or by soaking them in water, until the woody parts of their stalks begin to rot.

After the retted plants have been dried, they are fed into a *scutching* machine, which removes the seeds and breaks the rotted stalks in many places. The outer bark and inner pith are scraped away by blades, freeing the fibers. The flax fibers are then sent to mills where they are combed, spun into yarn, and woven into cloth.

Worker at a scutching machine

Dried flax

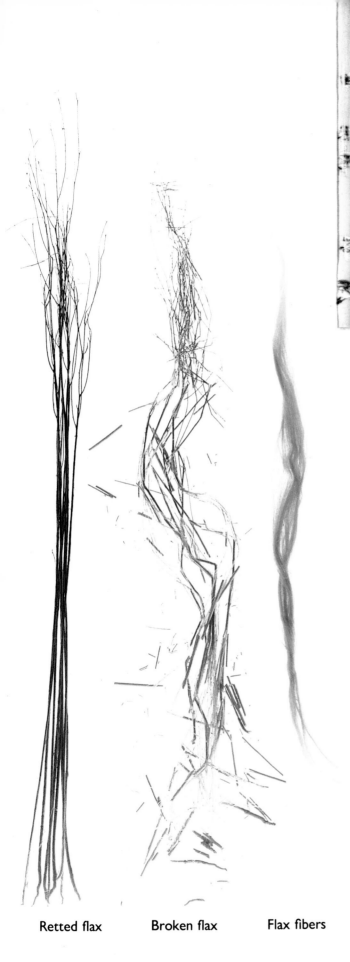

Drawing of
an enlarged
flax fiber

Under a microscope the flax fiber looks like a tiny stalk of bamboo. There are joints along the fiber, and it is hollow.

The outside of the flax fiber is smooth. This slick surface means that linen does not often shed tiny bits of its fiber, called lint. When you dry dishes with a linen towel, your glasses and plates will have less lint on them and look cleaner than if you used a cotton towel.

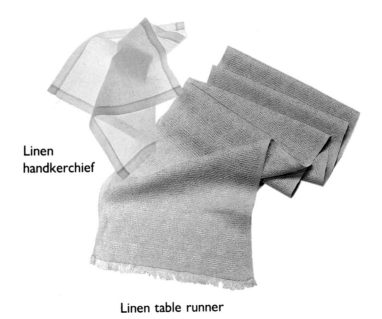

Linen
handkerchief

Retted flax   Broken flax   Flax fibers   Linen table runner

COTTON

There are so many things made of cotton that it would be hard to go through a day without using or wearing cotton cloth. You probably sleep between cotton sheets and wash your face with a cotton washcloth. Your shirts, jeans, socks, and even your shoestrings are often made of cotton.

Cotton shirt

Cotton grows best where it stays warm and sunny for at least half the year. Large amounts of cotton are grown in the southern United States, the southern part of the former Soviet Union, and in India. Farmers plant cottonseeds in the spring. When a cotton plant is about two months old, it begins to bloom.

There are flowers, and open and closed bolls growing on this cotton plant.

White flower

The white flower turns pink.

Dried flower on the tip of cotton boll

Open cotton boll

Each flower on a cotton plant is creamy white at first. Then the flower turns pink, and finally red. After three days, it dies, and the dry brown flower is pushed out on the tip of a new, green cotton *boll.* A cotton boll is a seedpod. Over several months, it grows to about the size of a Ping-Pong ball. Inside the boll, moist cotton fibers are forming around the cottonseeds.

By early fall the cotton plants are four feet tall. Most of the bolls have turned brown and popped open to show their cotton. The cotton fibers begin to dry and fluff out.

Over thirty seeds are hidden in the fibers of each boll.

Cotton picker unloading into trailer

Now it's time for the farmers to pick cotton. Giant picking machines run from sunrise until after dark. Clouds of cotton lint float around the pickers. The air is filled with the rich smell of freshly picked cotton.

Farmers haul trailers loaded with picked cotton to a *gin*. A cotton gin is a huge, noisy machine that pulls the cotton fibers away from the seeds. Other machines clean and dry the cotton. The clean cotton is bundled in five hundred-pound bales. The baled cotton is sent to mills to be made into cloth.

Cotton gin

Cotton picker picking cotton

Brown cotton

Green cotton

Although most cotton fibers are white, they can also be brown or green.
The brown and green cotton fibers become deeper in color after they are washed.

More things are made of cotton than any other fiber. One reason is because it costs less to harvest cotton fibers than most other fibers used to make cloth. Another reason is because cotton has many desirable features.

A T-shirt made of white cotton, and a skirt made of green and brown cotton

Cotton fibers suck up moisture easily and dry quickly. Cotton fibers are soft and lightweight. Each inch long fiber has a couple hundred twists in it. The twists help make cotton stretchy. All of these qualities make cotton cloth feel light, cool, and comfortable.

Drawing of an enlarged cotton fiber

JUTE

Look for a brown pad under your living room rug. It may be made of jute. Check to see if there is burlap cloth stapled to the bottom of your couch. Look in your kitchen for burlap bags filled with rice, coffee beans, or peanuts. Burlap is woven jute cloth.

Jute carpet pad and burlap bags filled with rice and peanuts

Most jute is grown and harvested in the moist heat of Bangladesh, India, and China. Jute plants grow to be very tall. In three or four months they can reach twelve feet. When the petals of the tiny yellow jute flowers fall to the ground, workers know it's time to cut down the plants.

Freshly cut jute is stacked in bundles to dry. Then, like flax plants, the dried jute is retted. It is soaked in water for several weeks to loosen the fibers from their stalks.

Workers called *strippers* separate the fibers from the stalks by jerking them back and forth in water. The woody parts of the plants slip off and float away. The stripper is left holding jute fibers that range from five to eight feet long.

Jute plant

Bangladeshi strippers removing jute fibers

Jute fibers going to mill by oxcart

The fibers are sent to a mill. They may travel by truck, boat, or oxcart. At the mill the jute fibers are made into cloth or rope.

Even though jute fibers are of poor quality, there is more jute produced than any other natural fiber except cotton. Jute fibers are plentiful and cheap because there are millions of people hand-planting, weeding, and collecting jute for low pay.

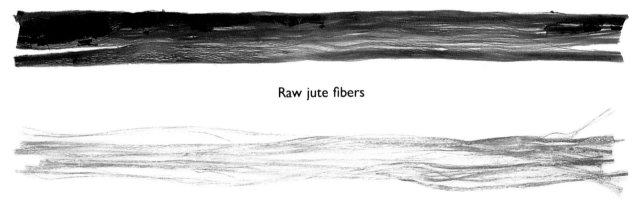

Raw jute fibers

Cleaned and combed jute fibers

Although items made of jute are found in many homes and stores, it is not well known. Perhaps this is because jute is made into things that are useful and not beautiful.

Dorset

WOOL

Wool comes from the thick, spongy fleece of a sheep. Sheep's wool comes in shades of black, white, and brown, and there are hundreds of different breeds of sheep.

In Asia, about eight thousand years ago, shepherds watched over the first flocks of sheep. Today sheep are raised all over the world. Australia, the former Soviet Union, and New Zealand have the largest numbers of them.

Once a year sheep are brought to the barn to have their fleece cut off, or *sheared.* The sheep huddle together, bleating loudly, as they wait their turn.

In the barn, the shearer sits a sheep on its rump. Using electric clippers, he trims along the sheep's belly and down one side. Then the shearer gently rolls the sheep to the floor to shear along its backbone. The sheep is seated again as the shearer clips the remaining side and peels off the fleece in a single piece. In five minutes the job is done and the sheared sheep is racing toward the field.

Shearing a sheep

Sheared sheep

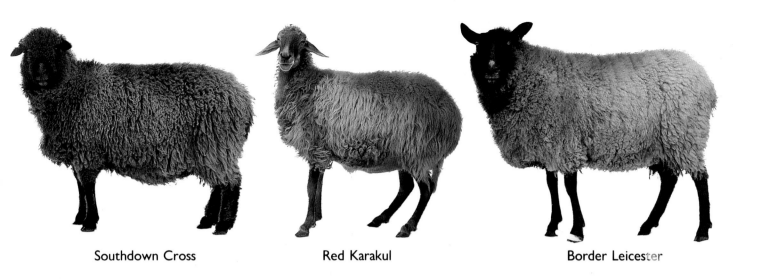

Southdown Cross   Red Karakul   Border Leicester

Notice the differences in the various breeds of sheep.

If you looked at a wool fiber under a microscope, you would see that the outside of the fiber is covered with scales. The scales on a wool fiber are like those on a fish. Water tends to run off them. The center of the wool fiber though sucks in and holds water.

When you wear a wool sweater, the perspiration from your skin gets pulled into the middle of the fibers. The wetness is kept away from your body by the fibers' scales. You feel warmer because your skin stays drier.

All animal hair commonly used to make cloth is covered with scales and sucks up moisture. But the wool fibers from sheep can hold more water away from your skin than any other kind.

Drawing of an enlarged wool fiber

Wool sweater and blanket

LLAMA AND ALPACA

For millions of years animals related to camels have lived in South America. These gentle creatures are smaller than camels and do not have humps on their backs.

Thousands of years ago, the people who lived in the Andes Mountains of South America tamed some of these animals. Over time, the offspring of these creatures developed into two new breeds of animals: llamas and alpacas. That is why all llamas and alpacas originally came from the areas now forming Bolivia, Chile, Argentina, and Peru.

Llamas are the size of big ponies. They are bigger and stronger than alpacas. Llamas can only carry about one hundred pounds when they are used as pack animals, and they don't carry people.

Llamas and alpacas are shy, yet curious. They hum softly except when they get angry; then they flatten their ears and spit!

Llama with packs   Alpacas

The fleece from both llamas and alpacas is used to make cloth, but alpaca is softer and fuller. It takes two years for llama and alpaca fleece to reach its full length of over a foot. People of the Andes Mountains cut the fleece from animals with large black scissors. In other places it is gathered by brushing or shearing off the fibers with electric clippers.

Llama and alpaca fibers are thick. They have the greatest diameters of all natural fibers that are used to make cloth. Many of these fibers have hollow centers, like tiny drinking straws. The thicker the fiber, the more likely its center will be hollow. The hollow fibers help keep bulky llama and alpaca clothes from feeling heavy.

Llama blanket

Alpaca vest

Alpacas

Clipping a llama with Andean scissors

ANGORA

Angora rabbits provide some of the finest, lightest, and warmest of all fibers. One of these rabbits weighs about as much as a small house cat but, because of its fluffy coat, looks twice as big.

Angora rabbit before plucking

Angora rabbits are named after a place in Turkey, where they came from hundreds of years ago. Today most Angora rabbits are raised in China and France. There are four breeds of Angora rabbits: English, French, Giant, and Satin.

Angora rabbits lose their hair when it reaches three to five inches in length. As they shed their fur, a second coat begins growing underneath. They can grow up to six coats a year!

Spinning yarn from an Angora rabbit

Shedding rabbit hair can be cut or *plucked*. Plucking is done by gently tugging on a small tuft of the rabbit's fur. The loose hair comes off easily. This does not hurt the rabbit, who sits quietly while its hair is gathered. Angora rabbits are so calm that spinners can hold the rabbits on their laps while they work, plucking fur and spinning it into yarn in a continuous motion.

Fibers from an Angora rabbit

Plucked Angora rabbit

Mittens and baby's hat made from one plucking of an Angora rabbit

The fluffy plucked coat of an Angora rabbit fills a grocery bag. Angora fibers are so light, however, that the bag seems empty. All of the hair in it would weigh only three or four ounces.

Wearing a knitted hat made of Angora rabbit's hair keeps your head much warmer than a hat of sheep's wool. One of the reasons why angora is so warm is that it is so fluffy. The fluff leaves air spaces between the fibers that trap and hold in the warmth of your body. Over time, the spun fibers of your angora cap will loosen and fluff up even more. The fluffier your cap gets, the warmer your head will feel.

Satin Angora

English Angora

French Angora

Giant Angora

MOHAIR

Angora goats, like Angora rabbits, once thrived in the place in Turkey known as Angora. But the white hair of Angora goats is called mohair.

The United States raises more Angora goats than any other country except South Africa. Most of the Angora goats in America live on ranches in the hills of western Texas. The warm, dry climate suits them, and they especially like to eat the bushes and grasses growing there.

Angora goats are frisky, nimble, and friendly, although they may butt each other when annoyed. Both does (female goats) and bucks have horns that they use for scratching and grooming.

Angora goat

Angora kid

Angora goat with a year's growth of mohair

Angora goats are not normally as big as other breeds of goats, but they are certainly hairier. An Angora goat's mohair grows one inch each month. If they are not sheared for a year, they grow mohair that falls in waves a foot long. Spinning mills do not work with such long locks, so most Angora goats are sheared twice a year.

Texans like to shear Angora goats "western style." Holding the goat by its horns, a shearer first clips the legs and belly, then ties the legs together, and shears the rest of the goat. Angora goats can also be tied to a special platform and clipped standing up.

Shearing an Angora goat on a platform

Goats under a year old are called *kids*. Kid mohair is fine and soft, and is made into lustrous sweaters and baby clothes. As Angora goats grow older, their fibers get thicker and rougher. The fibers of six-year-old, adult Angora goats are almost as thick as those of llamas. The coarsest mohair fibers are used to make carpets and upholstery.

You might have a special sweater made from the soft mohair of an Angora kid. If you have been to a symphony or ballet at a grand old theater, you might have sat on a seat covered in bristly mohair from an aging Angora goat.

Sweater made
from kid mohair

Seats covered in mohair at Carnegie Hall, New York City

CASHMERE

In the springtime a cashmere goat is covered with coarse hairs eight inches long. These, however, are not the cashmere fibers. This warm weather coat is made up of stiff fibers called *guard hairs*.

A cashmere goat with guard hairs

A cashmere goat with guard hairs and cashmere fibers

Combing a cashmere goat to remove the cashmere fibers

By the time winter's chilly weather settles in, the goat will have grown a second coat beneath the guard hairs to keep it warm. These fuzzy hairs, about two inches long, are the velvety cashmere fibers.

Each goat grows only a small amount of cashmere. It takes a lot of time to comb out the soft fibers, but this method allows them to be gathered without mixing in too many guard hairs.

Most cashmere goats are raised in China, Mongolia, and Iran. They are named after a place in India called Kashmir. There, hundreds of years ago, cashmere became famous for its use in shawls.

A cashmere overcoat is made from the fibers of more than thirty cashmere goats.

SILK

Rub a piece of silk cloth against your cheek. It feels soft and cool. No other cloth feels as smooth against your skin as silk.

The finest silk fibers are made by a special type of caterpillar called a silkworm. In ancient times, only the Chinese knew how to raise silk-worms. They kept it a secret for as long as they could. Today, China still raises more silkworms than any other country, but Japan, India, and South Korea also raise large numbers.

Silk wedding gown

Silkworms are raised on silkworm farms. They are hatched from eggs, each as small as the head of a pin. They prefer to eat only one food their whole lives: leaves from the mulberry tree.

Silkworm stages from eggs on a mulberry leaf to a fully grown caterpillar, actual size

Silkworms eating mulberry leaves

A silkworm eats constantly, day and night, until it becomes too big for its skin. Then the caterpillar breaks open its tight skin and wiggles out of it. There is a new skin underneath the old one. The old skin bunches up on the end of the silkworm and falls away. This process is called *molting*. A silkworm molts four times before it has finished eating. Each new skin is whiter and bigger than the one before, giving the silkworm more room to grow.

The head of
a silkworm

Silkworm molting

The whole time a silkworm is eating, it is making silk. The silk is created as a liquid inside two long, curly glands on either side of the silkworm's body.

After four weeks the silkworm stops eating. It has become a full-grown caterpillar.

The silkworms are then placed on frames to spin their silk. Each frame is divided into rows of open squares. The caterpillars, fat with silk, hunt around the frame, looking for a place to build their cocoons.

Soon each silkworm settles in to spin its silk. It does this by squeezing the liquid silk out of an opening in its head called a *spinneret*. The silk hardens when it touches the air, and becomes a fiber.

First the silkworm throws a web with its silk. It is not an orderly web like a spider makes. It is attached here and there to the walls of one square. The web anchors the silkworm's cocoon safely to the frame.

Balanced in the middle of the web, the silkworm builds a cocoon around itself. The caterpillar tosses its head from side to side in a figure-eight pattern as it puts out a thin fiber of silk. After a day you can't see the silkworm through the cocoon anymore, but it is still inside working. At the end of three days the cocoon is complete. Amazingly, it is made up of a single fiber of silk nearly a mile long!

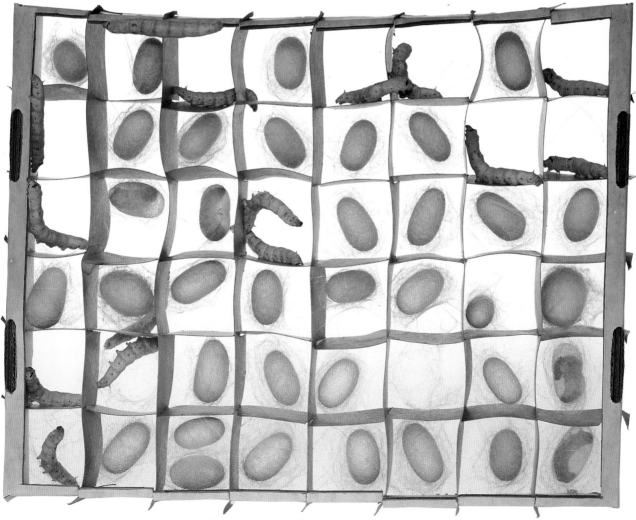

Some silkworms can still be seen inside their cocoons.

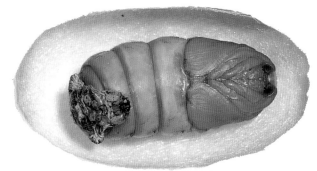
Silk moth chrysalis

The silkworm changes from a caterpillar into a chrysalis inside the cocoon. The chrysalis develops into a silk moth. After three weeks the silk moth spits out a liquid that breaks down part of the cocoon's wall. Then it pushes its way through the weakened area and out of the cocoon.

Only a few silk moths are allowed to escape from their cocoons to mate and lay eggs. This is because the hole a moth makes in its cocoon breaks the long silk fiber into many short ones. To keep this from happening, workers place most of the silkworm cocoons into ovens where heat or steam kills the chrysalis inside. This is called *stifling*.

A silk moth emerges from its cocoon.

Silk moths have wings but cannot fly.

Silkworm egg being laid

After mating with the male silk moth, the female lays from two hundred to five hundred eggs.

Unwinding cocoons by machine in China

Drawing of an enlarged silk fiber

The stifled cocoons are placed in hot water to loosen the silk fibers. A single silk fiber is too fine to be woven into cloth. Fibers from five to eight silk cocoons are unwound and pressed together into a single thread.

Silk fibers from six cocoons are pressed together into a single silk thread.

Silk thread is very strong. One thread as fine as a human hair can hold up to a pound of weight. Because silk is so strong, it has been used to make parachutes and ropes. Silk is also warm and lightweight, making it a good choice for long underwear.

A silk tie is made from the fibers of over one hundred cocoons.

Silk cloth looks shiny and bright because silk fibers are *translucent.* Light shines into them and spreads out inside them. They look like threads of frosted glass. People will pay high prices for silk because of its jewel-like translucence, and because it feels as good as it looks.

SYNTHETIC FIBERS

R A Y O N

Over one hundred and fifty years ago, scientists watched silkworms spin fibers after eating mulberry leaves and wondered if it was possible to create their own fibers from trees. The scientists began experimenting with mulberry trees and later with evergreen trees. In the late 1880s, the first man-made fibers used for cloth were produced. At first, these fibers were called artificial silk. Later, they were named rayon.

Rayon is made of *cellulose,* which is in the walls of all plant cells, and is the main substance of wood. To collect cellulose, pine, spruce, or hemlock trees are chopped up into small chips. These wood chips are cooked in chemicals and water to get an oozy pulp of wet cellulose. The pulp is bleached, squashed, and dried into thick white sheets. The sheets make it easier to transport the cellulose to a factory where they are transformed from a solid to a liquid. First, they are soaked in a strong chemical. Next, the soggy sheets are shredded into small white crumbs.

Pine tree   Wood chips   Thick sheet of cellulose   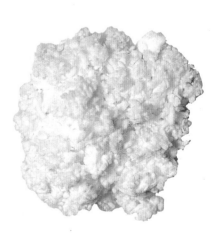 White crumbs

More chemicals are mixed into the crumbs, turning them orange, and then changing them into a gooey, honeylike liquid called *viscose.*

The viscose is pushed through a metal plate with many small holes. The plate is called a *spinneret,* named after the silkworm's spinneret. The viscose strands shoot out of the spinneret into an acid bath, where the liquid hardens into fibers. As the fibers leave the acid, they are twisted together into a single strand of yarn. After washing, the yellowish yarn turns white.

Rayon blouse

The size of the holes in a spinneret determines the fiber's thickness. Rayon fibers, like other synthetic fibers, can be thinner than the finest angora hairs or a hundred times thicker than the fattest llama fibers. The finest rayon fibers are used to make delicate, flowing dresses, while the thickest fibers are used in truck and airplane tires. The top three producers of rayon are Russia, Japan, and India.

Look closely to see many tiny holes in the spinneret.

On the left side of the picture, the yellowy viscose is going through a spinneret and into an acid bath. On the right side, look for the rayon yarn being pulled out of the acid.

Orange crumbs

Viscose is a thick, honey-colored liquid.

POLYESTER

All fibers are made up of *polymers,* but no one understood what a polymer was until 1920—over thirty years after the creation of rayon.

A molecule is the smallest part anything can be divided into and still exist by itself. Polymers are giant molecules. All molecules, even polymers, are too small to be seen even with the most powerful miscroscope. *Poly* means many, *mers* means parts, so polymers have many parts. Each polymer is a giant molecule formed by linking together hundreds of smaller molecules.

In time, chemists used their knowledge of polymers to try to make new ones. About sixty years ago chemists successfully created new polymers for fibers. Polyester, and most other synthetic fibers, are made from these newly invented polymers.

Although no one can see a polymer, chemists believe a polyester polymer is organized like this. Hydrogen (white), oxygen (red), and carbon (black) atoms form molecules that link together to make one long, giant molecule.

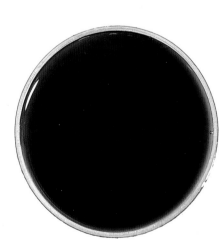

Petroleum is a rich soup of many chemicals.

Oil well

Polyester is made from two chemicals. One is called TPA and the other is glycol. They both come from petroleum, the crude oil found under the earth's surface. When TPA and glycol are heated together the small molecules containing hydrogen, oxygen, and carbon atoms link up to make a liquid of long polyester polymers.

The liquid is forced through a spinneret, and dries into fine polyester fibers as it hits the air. The fibers are stretched to make them stronger and much longer.

Polyester fibers being stretched

Polyester fibers being wound onto spools

The United States, China, and western Europe are the major producers of polyester. Polyester is the most common synthetic fiber found in clothes today. Clothes made of polyester are durable. This means they are tough. They will last longer than clothes made of most other fibers. Polyester clothes do not wrinkle easily. You do not have to iron clothes made of polyester after they are washed and dried. Chances are that at least one piece of the clothing you have on right now contains polyester.

Polyester dress

KEVLAR®

Kevlar gloves

No other fibers shield people from sharp edges and heat as well as Kevlar fibers. Many firefighters don coats containing Kevlar before putting out a fire. Race car drivers wear jumpsuits made with Kevlar to protect them against fiery crashes. In dangerous situations, police officers often wear bullet-resistant vests lined with layers of Kevlar cloth.

Like other fibers, Kevlar is made of polymers. However, the molecules used to make Kevlar, and the way these molecules are linked together, cause Kevlar to be stronger and more heat-resistant than other polymers. They also color Kevlar fibers bright yellow.

Go-cart driver wearing a jumpsuit made with Kevlar and other fibers

Polyester, and most other fibers, have polymers that can twist around and around into corkscrews. Curly chains of molecules get tangled up with each other. This weakens the fiber. Kevlar polymers are straight and stiff. When the straight chains of Kevlar molecules lie parallel to each other, they make a fiber that is much stronger than any other natural or synthetic fiber.

TCL has white crystals.

PPD is a pink powder.

Two chemicals, called PPD and TCL, are used to make Kevlar. They come from either natural gas or petroleum. Natural gas, like petroleum, is found underground.

PPD and TCL are blended in a special vessel, called a *reactor*. A thick syrup is formed. The syrup is made up of Kevlar polymers. In the reactor, the chains of molecules are jumbled together like a huge pile of pick-up sticks.

Kevlar reactor

Diagram of Kevlar polymers lining up in a fiber

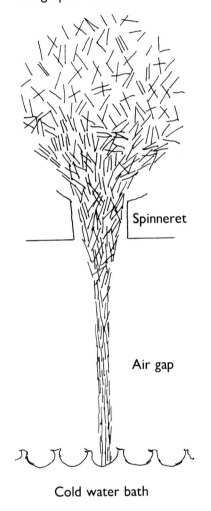

Spinneret

Air gap

Cold water bath

Kevlar syrup is yellow.

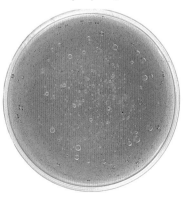

Kevlar fibers coming out of a spinneret and across an air gap

This syrup is pumped through a spinneret to make Kevlar fibers. As the syrup passes through the spinneret holes and across an air gap, the straight chains of molecules are forced to line up parallel to each other. Then the fibers are plunged into a cold water bath. When they come out of the water, they are strong, heat-resistant Kevlar fibers. Kevlar fibers are only made in the United States, Japan, and the Netherlands.

WORLD FIBER PRODUCTION

For thousands of years all of the fibers used to make cloth were natural fibers. Now, almost half of the fibers produced in the world are synthetic fibers made from trees, oil, and natural gas. Most of this change has taken place in the last fifty years.

FUTURE FIBERS

In the future, the fibers we use will continue to change. Some fibers will go out of fashion, while others will become more popular. Scientists will improve existing fibers and create new ones.

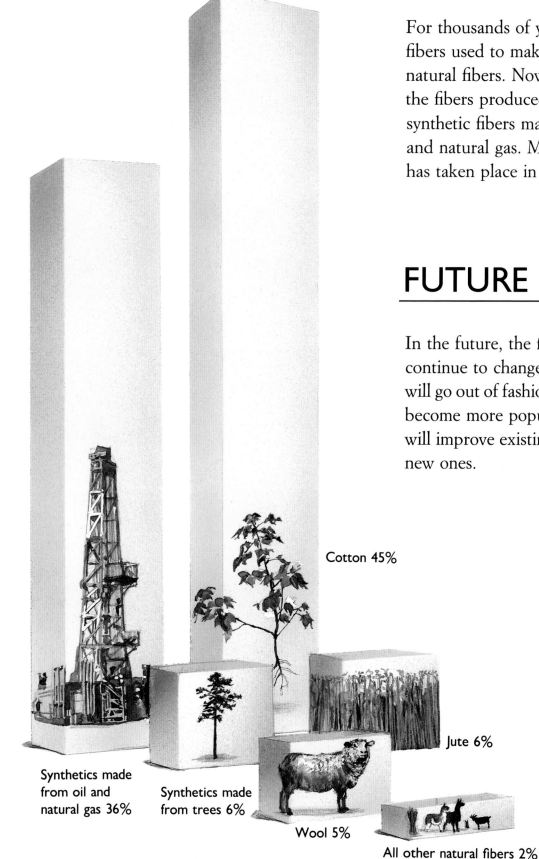

Cotton 45%

Jute 6%

Synthetics made from oil and natural gas 36%

Synthetics made from trees 6%

Wool 5%

All other natural fibers 2%

Current world fiber production

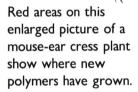

A mouse-ear cress plant shown actual size

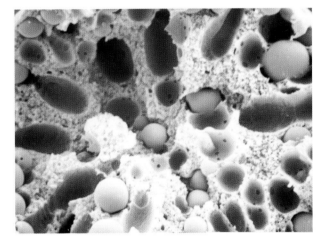

Red areas on this enlarged picture of a mouse-ear cress plant show where new polymers have grown.

Some of these changes are already happening. Selected genes have been put into tiny mouse-ear cress plants so that they are able to grow polymers like polyester. Unlike the polyester made from petroleum, however, the new plant-grown polymers are *biodegradable*. This means they can be easily broken down by nature. Soon scientists hope to produce such polymers in corn and potatoes.

Enlarged microcapsules

This picture shows the inside of a synthetic fiber enlarged two thousand times. You can see several microcapsules nestled in the fiber.

There are also specially treated fibers that capture heat from the environment or your body. The energy from the heat is held inside the fibers in microcapsules until the temperature drops. Then the microcapsules release the heat, through the fibers and back into the environment.

Ten years from now you may be wearing a shirt or pants made of polyester from a potato. Your jacket may store heat during the day, then use that heat to keep you warm at night. Imagine that!

INDEX

ACKNOWLEDGMENTS

The authors would like to thank the people who so generously gave their time to make this book possible, including Gladys Strong; Elton Nelson, Ph.D.; Roland Brierre, Ph.D.; Yvonne Bryant, Ph.D.; Robin Benson; Anita Okail; Robert Wooding; Michael and Betty Mann; David Vlaservich, Ph.D.; Khalil and Fatima Ahmed; Barbara and Gordon Tinder; Lyle Durrer; Betty and Hugh Whelchel; Annie Kelley; Barbara and Ranny Robertson; Jo Ann and Paige McGrath; Terry Bailes of Lanark; Jenny and Sherry Heath-Wagner; Britania Daniels; Teresa Bodde; Mabel Lighty; Donald McCall; Nancy Riddlemoser; Karen, David, and Ryan McNally; Judy Karow; Janice Bryce; Julie and Kevin Burns; Missy Scott; Gene and Rosalie Pendergrast; L. Rheinberg, M.B.E.; James Booterbaugh; Robert Dunn; Douglas Dennis, Ph.D.; Jonathan Monroe, Ph.D.; Susan Quel; Susan Senechal; Leslie Stanfield; and Betty Keeler. We would also like to thank the Museum of American Frontier Culture; International Linen Promotion Commission; Fiber Economics Bureau, Inc.; American Fiber Manufacturers Association, Inc.; E. I. du Pont de Nemours and Company, Inc.; BASF Corporation; Virginia Department of Mines, Minerals, and Energy; Vreseis Ltd.; Sajama Alpaca Yarns; Van Lear Bridals; Tiffany's Bridal Shoppe; Franco's; National Cotton Council of America; North American Rayon Corporation; Triangle Research and Development Corporation; James Madison University; and the Institute of Textile Technology.

Photo credits: Factory spinning (p. 3) and factory weaving (p. 3), both International Linen Promotion Comm.; factory knitting (p. 4), National Cotton Council; pulling machine (p. 5) and scutching machine (p. 6), both International Linen Promotion Comm.; cotton picker with trailer (p. 10), National Cotton Council; brown cotton (p. 11) and green cotton (p. 11), both Beth Brookhart; jute strippers (p. 12) and oxcart with jute (p. 13), both Elton Nelson; Carnegie Hall mohair seats (p. 21), Michael Legrand; unwinding cocoons (p. 27), L. Rheinberg; spinneret (p. 29) and rayon out of acid (p. 29), both North American Rayon; oil well (p. 30), DuPont; stretching polyester (p. 31) and polyester spools (p. 31), both American Manufactured Fibers Assoc.; Kevlar® reactor (p. 33) and Kevlar out of spinneret (p. 33), both DuPont; oil well (p. 34), DuPont; jute plants (p. 34), Elton Nelson; mouse-ear cress with polymers (p. 35), Yves Poirier of Michigan State University; microcapsules (p. 35) and microcapsules in fiber (p. 35), both Triangle Research and Development Corp.